For Ella and Riley

Published by The Ella Riley Group, Unit 1b, Stean Street Studios, 3-5 Dunston Road, London E8 4EH

www.davinahamilton.com

A catalogue record of this book is available from the British Library.

ISBN: 978-0-9957005-1-2

RILEY KNOWS HE CAN

Words by Davina Hamilton
Illustration by Elena Reinoso

Riley was nervous – today was the day;
He'd get on the stage in his first school play!
Riley was going to play a wise king
Who helped his kingdom to fix everything.

The king was a wonderful part to play,
And Riley had practised his lines every day.
But now that the day was finally here
Riley felt like he wanted to disappear!

His big sister Ella told him, "You'll be just fine.
Remember, I helped you to practise your lines!"
"I know," muttered Riley. "But what if I freeze?
Or what if I walk on the stage and I sneeze?"

"Relax," Ella told him. "Let's get one thing straight:
I know you can do this, you're going to be great!
You're clever and smart – you can be anything.
You're going to be the most wonderful king!"

Riley began to feel less in a muddle,
"Remember," said Ella, as she gave him a cuddle,
"If you start feeling nervous, this is the plan:
Say in your head, *'I can do this, I can!'*"

Riley didn't feel scared anymore.
He knew he could do it – in fact, he was sure!
Then Daddy appeared and said, "Time to go!
You can't be late for your first big show!"

Daddy walked Riley and Ella to school.
The sunshine was out, but the breeze made it cool.
"I'm so excited," Daddy said with a smile.
Riley, you'll be on stage in a while!"

Suddenly, Riley was nervous again –
His play was starting at 10 a.m.
But then he remembered his big sister's plan,
So he said in his head: *"I can do this, I can!"*

When they arrived at the big school gate
Ella said, "Good luck, Riley, you're going to be great!"
Daddy kissed Ella and said, "Have a good day!"
"I will," Ella said, as she ran off to play.

"How long 'til I'm on?" Riley wanted to know.
Daddy replied: "One more hour 'til the show!"
Then somebody shouted, "Riley, are you ready?"
Riley turned around – it was his friend Eddie!

Briiiiing went the bell, it was time to go inside.
Riley felt nervous – he wanted to hide!
But then he remembered his big sister's plan.
So he said in his head: *"I can do this, I can!"*

Daddy kissed Riley and said, "Good luck, son.
Go on the stage and have lots of fun!
Mummy and I will be cheering for you.
We'll sit at the front so we have a great view!"

Riley felt good as he ran into school.
He felt like a king who was ready to rule!
Into the classroom he went and sat down.
Then he spotted his costume – a cape and a crown!

Soon it was time for the children to go
Into the hall to prepare for the show!
Riley and Jamie and Tia and John
Were excited as they put their costumes on!

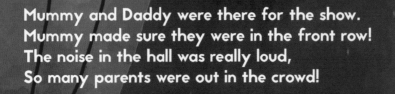

Mummy and Daddy were there for the show.
Mummy made sure they were in the front row!
The noise in the hall was really loud,
So many parents were out in the crowd!

Riley felt butterflies deep in his tummy,
He wanted to do well for Daddy and Mummy.
And then he remembered his big sister's plan,
So he said in his head: *'I can do this, I can!'"*

Onto the stage the children all ran –
The hall went quiet as the play began.
The first child to speak was Isabella:
She was the brilliant storyteller.

Isabella said loudly: "This is a tale
About the children of Grumpydale.
The children were always arguing;
Each of them thought they had the best thing."

Jamie said, "My shirt is the best."
Tia said, "I've got the prettiest vest!"
John said, "Look at my stylish sweater."
"No way," Lucy said. "My dress is much better!"

Isabella said, "The kids all huffed;
King Riley decided he'd had enough!
He gathered the children together one day,
And this is what he had to say."

"Children!" cried Riley. "Stop arguing!
All of you have wonderful things.
You mustn't fight, because that is wrong.
All of you must get along!"

Isabella said, "Riley the king,
Always knew how to fix everything."
Riley said, "Now, to end this tale,
I'm changing our town's name to Happydale!"

The play was finished – the children bowed.
Cheers and applause came from the crowd!
Mummy and Daddy looked so impressed –
Riley knew he had done his best!

When he got home after school that day,
Riley told Ella: "I was great in the play!
Whenever I'm nervous, I'll follow your plan.
I'll say in my head, *'I can do this – I can!'*"

Also from Davina Hamilton:

www.davinahamilton.com

Printed in Great Britain
by Amazon